STANLEY _{SM}

THE GREAT BIG BOOK OF EVERYTHING

By Ronne Randall

Disney PRESS

NEW YORK

Based on the "Stanley" books created by Griff with ticktock Entertainment Ltd.

Printed in Singapore
First Edition
1 2 3 4 5 6 7 8 9 10
Library of Congress Catalog Card Number: 2002110899
ISBN: 0-7868-3384-X

We would like to thank: Duncan Bolton at Bristol Zoo; the Entomology Department and the Bird Group (Department of Zoology) at the Natural History Museum, London; Isolde McGeorge at Chester Zoo; and Elizabeth Wiggans.

With special thanks to Lorna Cowan and Caroline Martin

CONTENTS

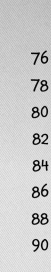

INTRODUCTION

Welcome to my **GREAT BIG BOOK OF EVERYTHING!** It's packed with strange and wonderful creatures from EVERY corner of the world—some you will know REALLY well, and others you may not have seen before!

Did you know that there are almost 2 million different kinds of animals on Earth?

MAMMAL

A furry coat

All the animals in my book have been divided into five different groups:

MAMMALS, BIRDS, REPTILES and AMPHIBIANS, UNDERWATER CREATURES (including fish), and BUGS AND SPIDERS.

Most mammals give birth to live babies, and then feed them milk from their own bodies. They mostly have furry or hairy coats, too! Birds are egg-laying animals with feathers.

REPTILE

Reptiles are creatures with thick, scaly skin. Most reptiles lay eggs, but some give birth to live babies. Amphibians are animals that live part of the time in water and part of the time on land, while fish (and the other underwater creatures) live in water all the time. Bugs and spiders live just about everywhere!

Mammals and birds are warm-blooded. This means their body temperature stays the same no matter how hot or cold the air or water is around them. Bugs, spiders, reptiles, amphibians, and fish are all cold-blooded. Their body temperature goes up and down depending on how hot or cold their surroundings are.

Thick, scaly skin

4

DO ALL ANIMALS EAT THE SAME STUFF?

Some animals, like lions or sharks, only eat meat or fish—they are called **carnivores** (you will see the symbols on the right next to their names). Others, like reindeer and elephants, only eat plants—they are called **herbivores**. Some animals, like grizzly bears and raccoons, eat plants and meat (or fish)—they are called **omnivores**.

Symbols to look out for:

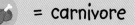 = carnivore

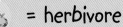 = herbivore

= omnivore

SOME BAD NEWS

Many of the world's wild animals are **endangered**. Sometimes it is because too many of them have been killed by hunters, or because they have been captured by people who want to sell them as unusual pets. Often it is because the places where they live, their habitats, have been destroyed. People chop down rain-forest trees so that they can sell the wood, and farmers dig up the land where wild animals live to grow food for their own families.

Endangered!

SOME GOOD NEWS

There are ways to help endangered animals, though—this is called **conservation**. Many governments have passed laws that ban hunting, and in some countries special parks have been created where endangered animals can live in safety.

People are animals, too. We are mammals—just like our cousins the apes. It is up to us to help look after our world and ALL the animals we share it with!

Now turn the page to see some COOL creatures. . . .

5

Any words that look bold, **like this**, are explained in the glossary at the back of the book.

BIG CATS

With really <u>BIG</u> teeth!

Cats have amazing eyesight and hearing. They are **carnivores**, so they only eat meat. Their coats can be striped or spotted, helping them to hide. This is called **camouflage**.

CHEETAH

Big cats play, too!

Cheetahs use their long tails for balance while they are running.

Over short distances, cheetahs can run over 70 mph! They are the world's fastest land animal.

After chasing and catching its **prey**, the cheetah needs about 30 minutes to get its breath back before it can eat.

6

TIGER

Tigers are the biggest cats of all. They are very strong!

ROAR!

Tigers love to cool off in the water and are excellent swimmers.

Time for a bath!

Each tiger has its own special pattern of stripes. Like human fingerprints, the stripes are all different.

HOW BIG ARE THEY?

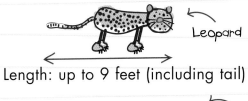

Cheetah

Length: up to 7 feet (including tail)

Leopard

Length: up to 9 feet (including tail)

Tiger

Length: up to 12 feet (including tail)

LEOPARD

Leopards can jump 13 feet high without even trying!

They are very good at climbing, and will often hide their food in trees.

Time to relax

Some leopards are very dark. It is hard to see their spots, but they are still there!

Can you spot the spots?

7

LIONS

Lions live in family groups called "prides." They are the only big cats that live in groups as adults. Prides normally have about four to six adult members. All the females in a pride are related, and they help to look after one another's babies.

LION

Most of the world's lions live on the grasslands of Africa.

Baby lions are called cubs.

When male cubs are about 18 months old, they start to grow a thick "mane" of hair around their head.

Lions are the only cats with manes and tufts at the end of their tails.

8

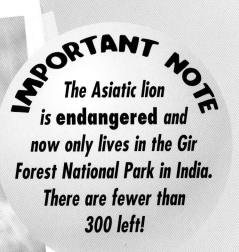

Look at those teeth!

Lion language is made up of lots of different growls: from low, rumbly grumbles to mighty ROARS that can be heard up to 5 miles away!

Grrrrrr

LIONESS

HOW BIG ARE THEY?

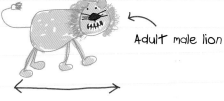
→ Adult male lion

Length: 10 feet (including tail)
Weight: up to 525 pounds

→ Adult female lion

Length: 8½ feet (including tail)
Weight: up to 395 pounds

Lioness—no mane

Lions will hunt anything from hares to hippos, but their main **prey** are antelope, zebras, and buffalo.

Lions spend a lot of time sleeping. They snooze for up to 20 hours each day.

Lions can't run for long distances; they usually creep up on their prey and then POUNCE on them! Lions hunt as a team, but the lionesses do most of the work.

9

THE DOG FAMILY

Good hearing and SHARP teeth!

Wolves, foxes, and pet dogs are all members of the same family. In the wild, dogs and wolves live in groups called "packs." A male and female pair leads the pack, and they are the only pair to have puppies. All members of the dog family have a very good **sense** of smell, which helps them find food.

SNIFF! SNIFF!

BLOODHOUND

Picking up the scent

Domestic dogs have been trained by humans to herd other animals, guard buildings, rescue people, and even do police work!

Bloodhounds' noses are 60 times more powerful than those of other dogs, and a million times more powerful than yours!

Bloodhounds can follow scents in heavy rain, and in temperatures below zero or as high as 99°F.

Bloodhounds can help the police track lost people. Their **sense** of smell is so good, they can smell a person's scent from fingerprints on a soda can.

WOLF

Most wolves live in cold places. To keep warm, they have a thick coat made up of two types of hair—a woolly undercoat and an outer layer of "guard hairs."

Large, sensitive ears

Wolves howl to one another to keep in touch. Each pack has its own song. The sound of their howls can travel for miles.

HOWL

Hunting as a pack, wolves can catch large **prey** such as reindeer and even moose.

HOW BIG ARE THEY?

Wolf

Height: up to 2 feet 10 inches (to the shoulder)

Bloodhound

Height: up to 2 feet (to the shoulder)

Red fox

Height: up to 20 inches (to the shoulder)

RED FOX

The red fox lives in forests and likes to hunt in nearby open fields. It is often seen by farmers in their fields.

Foxes hunt rabbits, birds, mice, beetles, and frogs. They also eat fruit.

This bushy tail is called a "brush."

The red fox is the largest of all the foxes.

11

J ANIMALS WITH POUCHES

Animals with pouches are called **marsupials**. They give birth to very, very tiny babies that are blind and have no hair. **Marsupial** babies crawl into their mother's pouch where they can feed and grow until they're big enough to go out into the world!

Mostly from Australia

RED KANGAROO

Red kangaroos are the largest of all the **marsupials**. They live in family groups called "mobs."

Kangaroos move by hopping on their big, powerful back legs, using their tails for balance. They can move at more than 30 mph!

During the daytime, when it's hot, kangaroos sleep in the shade, but in the cooler late afternoon and evening, they come out to eat their favorite food—grass.

Mom and baby kangaroo

The joey (baby kangaroo) stays in its mom's pouch for about six to eleven months!

TASMANIAN DEVIL

The Tasmanian devil's jaws are very powerful!

They hunt at night!

They were given the name "devil" by people who were frightened by their snarling barks and high-pitched shrieks.

HOW BIG ARE THEY?

Red kangaroo

Height: up to 5 feet

Koala

Length: 2 feet 8 inches

Tasmanian devil

Length: up to 2 feet 8 inches

KOALA

Koalas live in trees—eucalyptus trees are their favorite! They mostly feed at night and will eat more than a pound of eucalyptus leaves during their nightly feast.

The koala's habitat is now in danger! The trees where it lives are being cut down to make room for farms, roads, and buildings.

Koala paws are especially good for gripping and climbing. Koalas even sleep up in the treetops.

13

APES

Apes belong to an animal family called **primates**. People are **primates**, too, and apes are our closest animal relatives. Apes even look a bit like us, but they are MUCH hairier!

ORANGUTAN

Orangutans live in rain forests. Their name means "man of the forest."

Arms can span more than 6 feet!

They have very long, strong arms—just right for swinging through the treetops, looking for fruit.

Adult orangutans live on their own. Each night they make a new nest of leaves and branches to sleep in.

14

Gorillas are the biggest of all the **primates**. An adult male (like this one) can weigh up to 400 pounds.

IMPORTANT NOTE
Because of habitat loss and hunting, gorillas, orangutans, and chimpanzees are all now seriously endangered.

GORILLA

Gorillas live in family groups of up to twenty members. They search for food (leaves, plant stems and shoots, roots, and fruit) together.

Each family is led by an adult male. He protects the females and babies and is called a "silverback."

The hair on a male gorilla's back turns a silver color when he is about ten years old.

Gorillas make a kind of barking cough when they're upset and a purring "mmmm" sound when they're happy.

HOW BIG ARE THEY?

Gorilla → Height: up to 5 feet 6 inches

Orangutan → Height: up to 4 feet 6 inches

Chimpanzee → Height: up to 4 feet 6 inches

CHIMPANZEE

Clever chimpanzees can use tools. They poke sticks into termite nests, then pull them out and lick off the tasty termites.

They live in **BIG** groups.

Chimps mainly eat fruit, leaves, and seeds, but sometimes they hunt for birds and small monkeys! In captivity, chimps can live to be more than 50 years old.

15

MONKEYS

Very smart with good memories!

Monkeys walk on all fours.

Monkeys are **primates**, just like apes and people. You can tell monkeys and apes apart because most monkeys have tails—apes never do.

SNOW MONKEY

Snow monkeys actually make little balls of snow with their hands, then roll them along the ground to make snowballs! Some snow monkeys warm up in pools of water that are heated by hot, underground springs.

Snow monkeys (or Japanese macaques) live in "troops" of 20 to 30 animals in the forests and mountains of Japan.

MANDRILL

Males have colorful faces and a purple bottom! This makes them very handsome to female mandrills.

The BIGGEST monkey of all!

During the day, noisy groups of mandrills search for food on the ground: fruit, seeds, eggs, and small creatures. At night, they sleep in trees.

A mandrill's cheek pouches can hold a large amount of food, leaving feet and hands free for running.

Snow monkeys eat leaves and flowers in spring, fruit in autumn, and tree buds and bark in winter. They also eat crabs and grasshoppers!

HOW BIG ARE THEY?

Height: up to 2 feet 8 inches — Mandrill

Tail: $2^3/4$ inches long

Height: 2 feet 4 inches — Snow monkey — Thick, furry coat

Tail: 4 inches long

Capuchin monkey
Tail: 20 inches long

Length: up to 18 inches (not including tail)

CAPUCHIN MONKEY

Capuchin monkeys live in the rain-forest treetops; they only come down to the ground to drink. Their strong, flexible tails can hold on to branches and help them keep their balance.

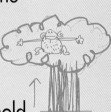

Capuchins eat fruit, seeds, and nuts, but they also like to eat **insects**, spiders, oysters, and even tree frogs! They live in groups of 8 to 14.

17

Good at climbing trees

BEARS

Bears are big, heavy, shaggy-coated mammals. Their eyesight and hearing are not very good, but with their large snouts, they have an excellent **sense** of smell.

GIANT PANDA

The giant panda is one of the world's most **endangered** animals. There are fewer than 1,000 left in the world.

Baby pandas are pink and hairless when they are born. They only weigh about 3^1/$_2$ ounces—Mom can weigh more than 220 pounds!

Pandas eat bamboo, a kind of tough, woody grass.

GRIZZLY BEAR

When a grizzly bear stands up on its back legs, it can be 13 feet tall! Grizzlies do this to threaten enemies and to look for food.

Over short distances, grizzly bears can run about 35 mph.

Grizzly bears are a type of brown bear. They can be fierce if they feel they are in danger, but are usually peaceful and like to be left alone.

Salmon for dinner!

They mostly eat plants, but will also eat meat and fish. In winter they snuggle down to sleep in a den until spring. This is called **hibernation**.

HOW BIG ARE THEY?

Giant panda

Length: up to 6 feet long

Grizzly bear

Length: up to 8 1/2 feet long

Polar bear

Strong swimmer!

Length: up to 10 feet long

POLAR BEAR

Polar bear paws are **webbed** for swimming and have furry pads for gripping the ice.

Polar bears are the biggest, land-living **carnivores** in the world. They hunt for seals and walruses in the sea and on the ice.

They have black skin.

Their fur looks white, which is good **camouflage** in the snow and ice, but each hair is actually a see-through, hollow tube. The clear hairs reflect the sun's light, which is what makes polar bears look white!

19

WEB-FOOTED ANIMALS

Animals that spend most of their time in the water are called **aquatic**. They have thick, waterproof fur to keep them warm in the water, and **webbed** hind or front feet to help them swim.

Ducklike feet

AMERICAN BEAVER

Beaver families live in "lodges" built from sticks held together with mud.

A flat, scaly tail

Beavers use their strong teeth to cut down trees for building dams (large barriers) in the streams where they live.

Water builds up behind the dam, creating a protective moat around the lodge and a safe, underwater place for storing tasty branches.

SEA OTTER

Sea otters enjoy shellfish like clams and shrimp. Holding a rock on their chest, they float on their back and crack open the shell on the rock!

They live alone.

PLATYPUS

When the first platypus was brought to England from Australia more than 200 years ago, people thought it was a fake animal.

No one could believe that a real animal could have a bill and webbed feet like a duck, and fur and a tail like a beaver.

The platypus lays eggs, like a bird or reptile, but feeds its babies milk because it is a mammal. Adults eat crayfish, worms, snails, and shrimp.

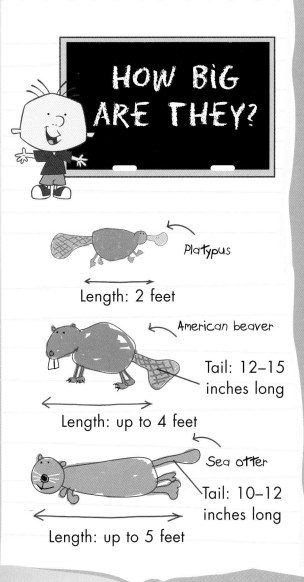

HOW BIG ARE THEY?

Platypus
Length: 2 feet

American beaver
Tail: 12–15 inches long
Length: up to 4 feet

Sea otter
Tail: 10–12 inches long
Length: up to 5 feet

A delicious shrimp dinner!

Sea otters love to groom one another. They have the animal kingdom's thickest fur.

Sometimes, before sea otters go to sleep, they wrap themselves in kelp (a type of seaweed); this keeps them in one place and stops them from drifting out to sea!

21

SPIKY ANIMALS

Porcupines and hedgehogs both have spiny coats, which help protect them from **predators**. They look alike, but are different in lots of ways.

Have ~~twills~~ ~~twills~~ quills

HEDGEHOG

Hedgehogs have whiskers and long snouts, which help them find the **insects**, slugs, and worms that they love to eat.

A scared hedgehog curls up into a tight, spiky ball—making it very difficult for an enemy to attack it!

Their thick, spiny coat has up to 7,000 spines.

This looks cozy!

During winter some hedgehogs that live in cold places have trouble finding food. They snuggle under piles of dead leaves and **hibernate** (sleep) until springtime.

22

PORCUPINE

Porcupines can have up to 30,000 quills. When they lose one, a new one grows in its place.

The porcupine's front teeth keep growing all its life. It has to gnaw on hard things to wear its teeth down.

Porcupines like to chew bark and eat leaves, buds, twigs, berries, and nuts.

This North American porcupine can climb trees!

Some porcupines can climb trees, while others live in underground tunnels.

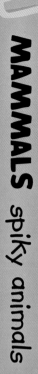

HOW BIG ARE THEY?

North American porcupine

Length: up to 3 feet

Western European hedgehog

Length: 9–11 inches

Porcupines have a woolly undercoat and an outer coat of soft guard hairs between their spiky quills.

When a porcupine gets scared, its quills stand on end. The quills can be dangerous. If they pierce the skin, it is very difficult to get them out.

So if you see a porcupine, don't frighten it and don't get too close!

SEALS, SEA LIONS, and others

Mammals that spend most of their time in the sea are called **marine** mammals. Manatees stay in the water all the time, but seals, sea lions, and walruses spend some time out of the water.

Love swimming and sunbathing!

SEA LION

California sea lions are clever and very playful! They can use their flippers to move about on land.

They gather on land in groups called **colonies**. Fish and squid are their favorite foods.

Sea lions have short, stubbly hair rather than fur.

Their favorite food is fish, fish, and more fish!

WALRUS

Male walruses have long **tusks** that are actually teeth. The tusks can grow up to 3 feet long.

Walruses can stay underwater for 25 minutes! They use their **tusks** to root around for shellfish, snails, and worms on the seabed.

Walruses also use their **tusks** to help pull themselves out of the water. This is very useful, as a male walrus can weigh almost 4,000 pounds!

SEAL

Some seal pups born in icy, snowy places like the Arctic have white fur to **camouflage** them.

A harp seal pup

Seals like to laze in the sun, but are clumsy when they move on land or ice. In the water they are fast and graceful.

Many seals live in cold water. Thick fur and a layer of **blubber** keep them warm.

MANATEE

Manatees are gentle, slow-moving animals. They eat lots and lots of underwater plants.

Many manatees are covered in scars from being hit by boats. They are also at risk from fishing nets and polluted water.

HOW BIG ARE THEY?

Seal (lots of different kinds)
Length: 4–18 feet

Sea lion (lots of different kinds)
Length: 5–10 feet

Walrus
Length: up to 10 feet

Manatee (West Indian)
Length: up to 16 feet

There are many old stories of sailors seeing mermaids. Nowadays, some people think that the creatures the sailors saw were actually manatees, who live close to the shore in shallow water.

25

DOLPHINS AND WHALES

Whales and dolphins belong to a family called **cetaceans**. They are mammals, so they don't have **gills** (like fish) and need to come above water to breathe through **blowholes** on the top of their heads. They speak to each other in whistles, groans, and squeaks.

The blue whale is the biggest creature living on Earth— it weighs as much as twenty elephants!

They feed their babies milk!

BLUE WHALE

No teeth!

A heart the size of a small car!

The blue whale is also the loudest animal on Earth. Its whistlelike call is louder than the sound of a jet plane.

Blue whales can eat up to 9,000 pounds of **plankton** (tiny sea plants and creatures) in a day. They suck in gallons of water, then filter out the food through special, bristly parts of their mouths called "baleen plates."

26

BOTTLENOSE DOLPHIN

Bottle-shaped beak

Bottlenose dolphins are actually small whales. They eat fish and shellfish.

Dolphins will chase a school of fish, circling nearer and nearer until the fish form a huge cluster. Then the dolphins dive into the middle to snap up a tasty meal!

Clever dolphins talk to each other using sounds and signs. They slap the water with their tails and leap into the air—as high as 20 feet!

HOW BIG ARE THEY?

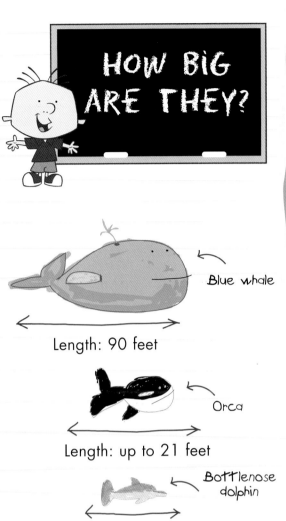

Blue whale
Length: 90 feet

Orca
Length: up to 21 feet

Bottlenose dolphin
Length: 10 feet

ORCA (KILLER WHALE)

See any food?

Orcas live in "pods" (family groups). Each pod has its own special language.

The male orca's "dorsal" fin can be 6 feet high.

Orcas eat squid and shrimp. They also are excellent hunters—they attack birds, seals, other whales, and even sharks!

Their black backs **camouflage** them in the water.

27

HIPPOS AND RHINOS

Rhinos and hippos both look a bit fierce, but they actually only eat plants—not other animals. Still, they will attack anyone who threatens them, and hippos are one of the most dangerous animals in Africa!

HIPPOPOTAMUS

"Hippopotamus" means "river horse" in ancient Greek (a language from long ago).

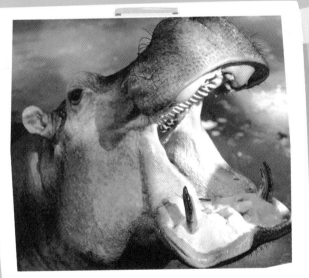

Open wide!

Hippos have HUGE teeth that keep growing all their lives. Males use them when they are fighting over females.

Hippos spend almost all day in the water lazing around and eating water plants. At night they come out onto land and graze on grass and reeds.

Hippo sweat is pink or red! It has special substances to cool down the hippo and keep its skin healthy.

Huge and very HEAVY

Rhinos need to eat huge amounts of grass, twigs, and leaves every day.

RHINOCEROS

There are five different kinds of rhinos: Indian, Black, White, Sumatran, and Javan.

Rhinos have bad eyesight, but a good **sense** of smell and good hearing.

Their horns are made of a tough stuff called "Keratin" mixed in with hair. Keratin is in your hair and fingernails, too.

HOW BIG ARE THEY?

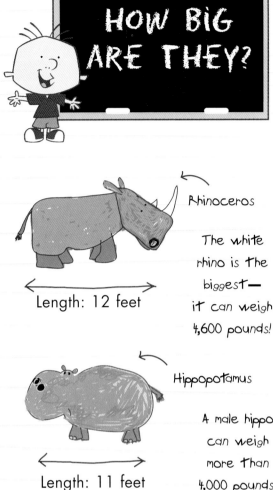

Rhinoceros

Length: 12 feet

The white rhino is the biggest— it can weigh 4,600 pounds!

Hippopotamus

Length: 11 feet

A male hippo can weigh more than 4,000 pounds!

CHARGE!

IMPORTANT NOTE

So many rhinos have been killed for their horns that they are now **endangered**. People kill them because they falsely believe that crushed-up rhino horn can cure illnesses. Rhinos are also losing their habitat as humans move in to the areas where they live.

Rhinos will CHARGE at anything (or anyone) that startles them.

29

ELEPHANTS

Elephants are the largest animal that lives on land. There are two different kinds: African elephants and Asian elephants. African elephants are slightly larger than Asian elephants and have much bigger ears.

Grass for lunch again

Elephants live on savannas and in forests. They can eat up to 450 pounds of bark, leaves, branches, and grass in a single day.

Elephants' trunks are not just for smelling: the animals use them to pull down trees, pick up food, suck up water, and spray protective dust over their backs when they get hot.

Elephants cannot run or jump, but they can walk very fast.

Sensitive little "fingers" at the tip of the trunk can help an elephant pick a feather off the ground!

Elephants can live to be 70 years old!

30

Elephants drink almost 50 gallons of water a day— enough to fill a bathtub!

They are good swimmers, and can use their trunks like snorkels.

Elephant herds are made up of related females and their babies. When males grow up, they leave the herd.

HOW BIG ARE THEY?

Height: up to 11 feet (to the shoulder)

African elephant

Weight: 12,000 pounds

Height: 10 feet (to the shoulder)

Asian elephant

Weight: more than 10,000 pounds

Baby elephants suck their trunks.

IMPORTANT NOTE

Adult elephants only have one enemy—humans! For many years they were killed for their tusks, but this is now against the law. However, elephants are still in danger; as more and more humans move into the areas where elephants live, they are losing their habitats.

Elephants are good mothers and aunts: they will crook their trunk around a baby's bottom to help it climb a steep hill, and shelter it under their bodies from the hot sun. All the members of a herd will protect a baby from **predators**.

31

GIRAFFES AND CAMELS

Camels and giraffes both have special stomachs that let them chew up their food, swallow it, and then when it is in their stomach, burp it back up and eat it all over again—to get maximum nutrition out of it!

Eat leaves and bushes

 ## GIRAFFE

Hundreds of years ago, the Romans called giraffes "camelopards." They thought they were camels with leopard spots.

Amazing patterns!

Their long legs, neck, and tongue help them reach leaves at the tops of trees. A giraffe's tongue can be 18 inches long!

Giraffes can eat up to 70 pounds of leaves a day.

When giraffe calves are born, they are already nearly 6 feet tall.

Giraffes are the tallest animals in the world!

32

DROMEDARY

Has one hump

Camels survive by storing fat in their humps. This gives them energy.

There are two types of camel: dromedaries and Bactrian camels. They both live in places where there is normally not much food or water, such as deserts and mountains.

HOW BIG ARE THEY?

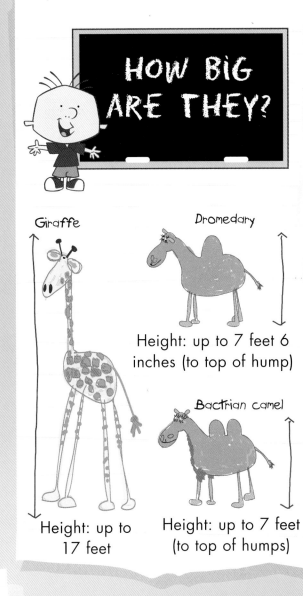

Giraffe

Dromedary

Height: up to 7 feet 6 inches (to top of hump)

Bactrian camel

Height: up to 17 feet

Height: up to 7 feet (to top of humps)

BACTRIAN CAMEL

Camels can go for almost two weeks without water, then drink up to twenty-five gallons in one sitting!

Has two humps

Camels have two rows of eyelashes to protect their eyes during sandstorms. They can also close their nostrils to keep out sand.

Bactrian camels have shaggy coats.

33

FARM ANIMALS

Farm animals such as cows, goats, and pigs are raised to give us milk and meat. We also use their skin for leather, and their woolly coats for making cloth.

WILD BOAR

COW

Cows eat grass and chew their "cud" (food that they have already eaten and burped back up) for up to eight hours every day!

Before she can start producing milk, a cow must have a calf (a baby).

Dad is called a bull.

YAK

Tibetan people get milk and meat from yaks. They use their skins to make tents, and their hair to make rugs and ropes.

Yaks are shaggy mountain cousins of cows.

Yaks eat grass, moss, and herbs. If there is no water high up in the mountains, they crunch up ice.

GOAT

There are many different species of goats. Some live on farms, and others are wild.

A dairy (milking) goat

Angora goats have hair that can be made into a soft, silk wool called "mohair.

PIG

Farm pigs and wild boars are cousins.

Lives in a farm pen

HOW BIG ARE THEY?

Wild boars live in forests and have hairy, bristly coats. They are fast runners and good at swimming.

Their long snouts and **tusks** help them dig up the plant roots and bulbs they like to eat.

Yak

Height: 6 feet (to the shoulder)

Cow

Height: 5 feet (to the shoulder)

Goat (farm goat)

Height: up to 3 feet (to the shoulder)

Ibex

Height: 3 feet (to the shoulder)

Pig

Boar

Height: 3 feet (to the shoulder)

IBEX

Goats can live in deserts or up in high mountains. They don't mind eating the scrubby plants that grow in these tough places.

Good climbers

Ibex are wild mountain goats that live in herds. They can climb quickly to avoid wolves and bears, or use their horns to fight them off.

HORSES AND ZEBRAS

Just one toe on each foot!

Horses and zebras both have long legs that help them run fast over long distances. People tamed horses more than 5,000 years ago, but zebras are still wild. They both eat grass, but tame horses are fed hay (dried grass) and get extra treats like carrots and apples!

HORSE

Male horses and zebras are known as stallions. Females are called mares, and their babies are called foals.

Foals can stand up and walk just an hour or two after they're born!

ZEBRA

Zebras live on the African plains.

They live in family groups made up of a stallion and several mares and their foals.

A zebra foal

Good **camouflage**

To **predators** like lions, that are color-blind, the zebra's stripes blend in with the tall grass, so the zebra becomes almost invisible!

Sometimes zebras join herds of antelopes, and they both help each other look out for enemies.

HOW BIG ARE THEY?

Horse

Height: 5 feet or 15 hands
(to the shoulder)
*ponies are 4 feet 7 inches or less

Zebra

Height: 4 feet 6 inches (to the shoulder)

A stallion

Horses normally sleep standing up, but they will lie down if they feel safe.

Horses' hooves are always growing, like our fingernails. Horses used for riding or work have their hooves trimmed. They also wear protective metal shoes on the bottom of their hooves.

Horses are measured in "hands." One hand is 4 inches, about the width of a grown-up's hand.

37

ANIMALS WITH HORNS

Deer and antelope are cousins. Adult male deer have bony **antlers** on their heads. The **antlers** fall off every year, and then grow back again. In the antelope world, both males and females have horns, which keep growing all their lives.

MOOSE

Moose like being near water. They will often wade into lakes to eat underwater plants.

When deer antlers are growing, they are covered with soft skin called velvet. It gets rubbed off on trees and in fights.

Moose are the biggest deer in the world.

38

REINDEER

In summer, reindeer eat grass and herbs. In winter, they use their hooves to dig under the snow to find fungus and moss to eat.

Reindeer are the only deer where both males and females have antlers.

People tamed reindeer about 7,000 years ago, but there are still many wild reindeer, too.

Domestic (tame) reindeer pull sleighs and are kept for their meat and skins.

HOW BIG ARE THEY?

Moose
Height: up to 6½ feet (to the shoulder)

Reindeer
Height: up to 4 feet (to the shoulder)

Pronghorn
Height: 3 feet (to the shoulder)

A thick coat keeps out the Arctic cold.

PRONGHORN

The pronghorn has horns like an antelope, but it sheds them every year, like a deer!

Pronghorns can run 40 mph and jump up to 20 feet in one leap.

ANTELOPE

Most antelope live in Africa. They come in lots of different sizes: from the smallest, the dik-dik (10 inches tall at the shoulder), to the BIGGEST, the eland (6 feet tall at the shoulder).

Antelope horns can be long, short, twisted, curved, or straight.

39

ANIMALS WITH FANCY TAILS

The bushy, striped tails of these animals make them easy to see in the forests where they live. A raised tail is a signal to friends, and warns enemies to keep away!

RACCOON

Nocturnal raccoons live in forests, but often come into towns to steal food from garbage cans.

They eat everything from insects, nuts, and berries to fish and frogs. With their skillful paws, they can even turn on water taps and open cans of soft drinks!

A mask like a bandit's

Raccoons often wash dirt off their food before eating it.

40

Ring-tailed lemurs spend time in trees and on the ground. They love to sunbathe.

RING-TAILED LEMUR

Groups of ring-tailed lemurs can travel up to 4 miles a day, searching for food—fruit, leaves, birds' eggs, and small animals.

When fighting over females, males rub their tails on special **scent glands** on their wrists. Then they have "stink fights" by flicking their tails at one another.

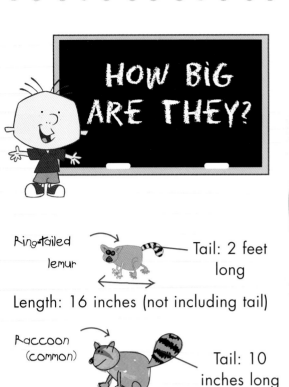

HOW BIG ARE THEY?

Ring-tailed lemur — Tail: 2 feet long

Length: 16 inches (not including tail)

Raccoon (common) — Tail: 10 inches long

Length: up to 2 feet (not including tail)

Striped skunk — Tail: 10 inches long

Length: up to 2 feet 6 inches (not including tail)

SKUNK

Skunks are best known for the nasty smell they give off. If an enemy is nearby, they stamp their feet, then do a warning handstand.

If the enemy doesn't leave, they spray a smelly liquid at it—the spray can reach as far as 10 feet!

Skunks love to eat people's leftovers!

41

ODD-LOOKING ANIMALS

These curious creatures may look strange to us, but their bodies are perfect for the places where they live. The sloth's big claws are just right for hanging in trees, and the anteater's long snout is great for slurping up insects!

Sniffy, slimy, and slurpy!

ANTEATER

Anteaters have long, tubelike snouts that are good at smelling out ant and termite nests.

Their strong, sharp claws rip ant and termite nests apart; then their sticky tongues lap up the insects.

A giant anteater can eat up to 30,000 ants and termites a day.

The giant anteater lives on the ground, but the silky anteater lives in trees and eats tree ants.

This sticky tongue is 2 feet long!

SLOTH

Sloths live in South America. They hang upside down in rain-forest trees, using their curved claws to hold on.

Green fur?

A sloth's favorite food is leaves—so everything it needs is up in the treetops!

Camouflage is important, because sloths move very slowly and are easily caught by **predators**.

Some sloths even have green **algae** (a sort of plant) growing in their coats—this helps to camouflage them.

HOW BIG ARE THEY?

Giant anteater

Length: 6¹/₂ feet (including tail)

Sloth

Height: 2 feet 2 inches

Nine-banded armadillo

Length: 22 inches (including tail)

ARMADILLO

Armadillo means "armored" in Spanish. Bony armor protects the animal from enemies.

A nine-banded armadillo

It has a long, sticky tongue for slurping up insects.

Nine-banded armadillos are good swimmers, and even walk along the bottoms of streams and ponds—underwater.

43

FLYING ANIMALS

Bats are the only mammals that have wings, and can actually fly. (Flying squirrels *look* as if they are flying, but they are really gliding.)

They are mammals, not birds!

BATS

FLYING SQUIRREL

The North American flying squirrel can leap off a high tree branch and then glide for more than 150 feet—landing in the lower branches of another tree.

Their favorite foods are acorns, nuts, berries, and seeds.

Flying squirrels have a flap of skin that joins the front and back legs—like a sort of parachute. They steer and change direction by turning their legs and flapping their tails.

44

Flying squirrels are **nocturnal**. Their big eyes are good for seeing in the dark.

Bats live in **colonies** in trees, holes in rocks, buildings, or caves.

During the day, they hang upside down to sleep; at night, they fly out to look for food.

Most bats eat **insects**. When hunting, the bats make high-pitched sounds. This is called "echolocation." Echoes from the sounds bounce off the insects, telling the bats where to find them.

This is a leaf-nose bat!

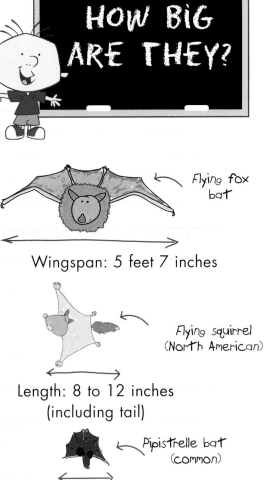

HOW BIG ARE THEY?

Flying fox bat

Wingspan: 5 feet 7 inches

Flying squirrel (North American)

Length: 8 to 12 inches (including tail)

Pipistrelle bat (common)

Wingspan: 10 inches

The flying fox bat is a type of fruit-eating bat. It finds fruit by using its **sense** of smell.

A flying fox bat

FAST-MOVING ANIMALS

These animals are very good at getting away from their enemies, either by running and hopping very quickly, or by escaping into their underground homes. All these animals eat grass and plants.

RABBIT

Some rabbits live in large groups in underground **burrows**.

When they are about to give birth, female rabbits dig a new **burrow** and make a nest out of leaves and their own fur.

The babies, called kittens, are born blind with no fur.

They stay close to their **burrows** so they can quickly escape from enemies.

JACKRABBIT

Jackrabbits are really a type of hare. They live aboveground and have their babies in a simple nest called a "form."

Hares are bigger and thinner than rabbits.

Strong back legs!

Hares can run very fast and can leap 5 feet in the air.

Jackrabbits have black tips on their ears.

Hares have longer ears and longer back legs than rabbits do.

PRAIRIE DOG

Prairie dogs live in underground **burrows** that are connected to form "towns."

Sometimes prairie dogs look like they're kissing, but they are really trying to recognize their friends by smell.

They disappear into their **burrows** at the first sign of danger.

HOW BIG ARE THEY?

Jackrabbit
Length: 20 inches

Rabbit
Length: up to 20 inches

Prairie dog
Length: 12 inches

Prairie-dog towns can stretch for miles!

47

ANIMALS WITH BIG FRONT TEETH

These little animals were all born to gnaw, bite, and chew on things! Their big, strong front teeth keep growing and growing, so they have to keep gnawing and gnawing to wear their teeth down.

They are all rodents.

There are more than 600 different kinds of mice.

MOUSE

House mice eat almost anything—even soap and glue!

Field mice prefer grains, fruit, insects, and grass.

SQUIRREL

Most squirrels live in hollows in trees or in nests called "dreys."

Their bushy tails help them balance in the treetops.

Squirrels bury nuts in the ground, then dig them up when food is scarce in winter.

Mice can have many litters of babies each year. It doesn't take long for two mice to turn into two hundred!

48

VOLE

Voles dig out little runways or networks of **burrows** under grass and crops, so farmers and gardeners don't like them.

Water voles live by rivers, lakes, and ponds. If it gets too crowded, they have noisy, squeaky fights until one group moves out!

SQUEAK SQUEAK SQUEAK

HOW BIG ARE THEY?

Groundhog
Length: 2 feet (including tail)

Squirrel (lots of different types)
Length: 12–15 inches (not including tail)

Mouse (common house mouse)
Length: 5 inches (including tail)

Vole
Length: 5 inches (including tail)

GROUNDHOG

Groundhogs eat seeds, roots, and plants. Their favorite food is clover.

Groundhogs dig long, deep **burrows** in empty fields.

In autumn, groundhogs eat a lot! They get very fat, ready to spend the winter in **hibernation**.

LIZARDS

Lizards are reptiles. They are related to snakes, but most lizards have legs, eyelids, and ear openings.

CHAMELEON

KOMODO DRAGON

The chameleon's tongue is longer than its whole body!

When an insect or spider passes by, the chameleon flicks out its long, sticky tongue and catches it.

The chameleon can change color to blend in with its background. This helps it hide from **predators**—and surprise its **prey**!

Each eye can move on its own. This means the chameleon can look in two different directions at once.

50

GECKO

Geckos can use their long tongues to clean their eyes.

Some geckos live around people. They are good pest controllers because they love eating bugs!

Geckos live in warm places.

Many geckos have tiny hairs on their feet, which help them climb up walls.

Female Komodo dragons dig out large burrows in sandy ground to lay their eggs in. After the eggs have **hatched**, the babies live in trees to avoid predators.

HOW BIG ARE THEY?

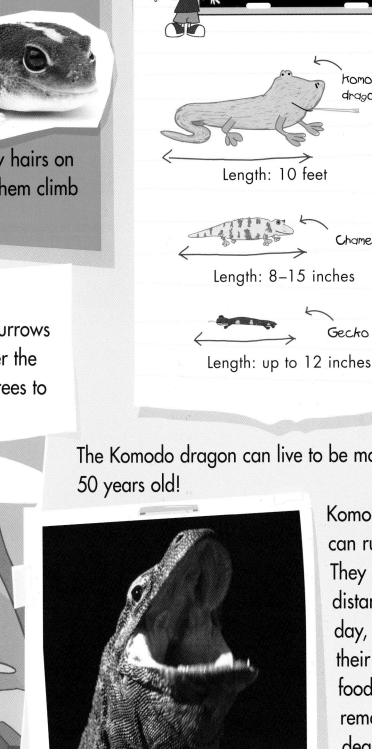

Komodo dragon

Length: 10 feet

Chameleon

Length: 8–15 inches

Gecko

Length: up to 12 inches

The Komodo dragon can live to be more than 50 years old!

Komodo dragons can run fast. They travel long distances every day, looking for their favorite food—the remains of dead animals.

world's largest lizard

51

CROCODILES AND ALLIGATORS

Alligators and crocodiles live in warm, tropical places near rivers and **swamps**. Some crocodiles can live in seawater, too.

World's biggest reptiles

CROCODILE

A hungry crocodile can be very dangerous to people. Thankfully, once a crocodile has had a large meal, it won't need to eat again for several weeks!

The African crocodile bird picks out bits of food and dead **insects** from the crocodile's teeth and gums. The bird has a good meal, and the crocodile gets clean teeth.

 Crocodiles and alligators hunt fish, turtles, birds, and mammals—even big ones! They can't chew, so they swallow small things whole.

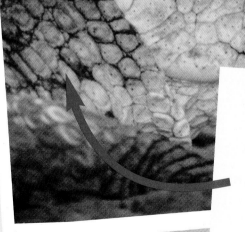

Ways to tell crocodiles and alligators apart:
- Crocs have a long, narrow snout.
- Alligators have a wide snout.
- You can see a croc's lower teeth when its mouth is shut.
- When an alligator's mouth is shut, you can only see its upper teeth.

52

Crocodile and alligator moms lay between 20 and 60 eggs at a time, in a waterside nest made from mud and leaves.

Crocodile and alligator mothers are very protective of their eggs and babies! When the eggs **hatch**, the mothers hear the babies calling and help them out of the nest.

HOW BIG ARE THEY?

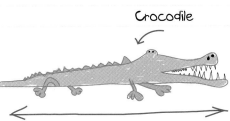

Crocodile

Length: up to 20 feet

Alligator

Length: up to 16 feet

ALLIGATOR

During dry times when there is not much rain, alligators use their tails and hind legs to dig the last of the water from the bottom of water holes. Then they lie in wait and catch the thirsty animals that come by for a drink.

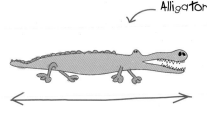

Alligators and crocodiles have between 60 and 80 teeth.

53

TURTLES AND TORTOISES

Turtles mainly live in the water, while tortoises live on land. They can both live to a very old age; there are records of tortoises living for more than 150 years!

The only reptiles with shells

TURTLE

A hawksbill sea turtle

Turtles have a sharp beak for cutting their food, but no teeth.

Many turtles eat sea creatures like jellyfish, sea urchins, and sea sponges. Others eat seaweed.

Turtles have **webbed** feet and a streamlined shell, to help them swim fast.

Mother turtles dig nest holes on sandy beaches. They lay their eggs in the holes, bury them, and then go back to the sea.

When the eggs **hatch**, the babies have to look after themselves. They need to get to the sea fast, before they are seen by **predators**.

Tortoises are herbivores. They eat grass and plants.

IMPORTANT NOTE

The hawksbill sea turtle is critically **endangered**. It is hunted for its shell (for jewelry making), and the beaches where it nests are disturbed by the building of hotels. Many other species of turtle are in great danger, too.

54

TORTOISE

A dome shape

Tortoise shells are high and domed. Their bodies store water and fat underneath the shell. Fat is also stored in their legs and tails.

HOW BIG ARE THEY?

Turtle

Length: 4 inches to 8 feet

Tortoise

Length: 9 inches (average size)

Giant Galápagos tortoise

Length: up to 4 feet 3 inches

Desert tortoises live in underground **burrows**. They can go for up to a year without water. They get all the moisture they need from the grass and wildflowers they eat in the spring.

If they live in a place that gets cold in winter, some tortoises will **hibernate** for several months.

55

SNAKES

They have Y-shaped tongues.

Snakes are cold-blooded reptiles with no legs. Most snakes cannot see very well, but they have a good **sense** of smell. Some snakes use their tongues to "taste" the air for the scent of their **prey**.

PYTHON

Pythons wrap their coils around their **prey**. Each time the trapped animal breathes out, the python tightens its grip until its victim stops breathing. Then the python swallows it—headfirst!

The reticulated python is the world's longest snake. It can grow to 30 feet long and weigh 350 pounds!

This is an African royal python, or ball python.

A group of snake eggs is called a "clutch." Pythons lay between 10 and 100 eggs at a time.

56 The reticulated python can swallow an animal as big as a deer—WHOLE!

COBRA

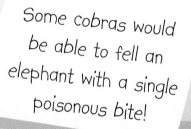

The king cobra is the world's biggest venomous (poisonous) snake.

Cobras have "hoods" of skin. They spread them to make themselves look bigger and extra scary.

Some cobras spit their **venom** at their prey (birds, small mammals, lizards, and other snakes), but most use their **fangs** to inject venom into their victims.

Some cobras would be able to fell an elephant with a single poisonous bite!

HOW BIG ARE THEY?

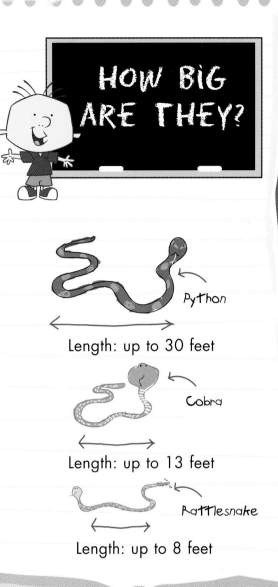

Python

Length: up to 30 feet

Cobra

Length: up to 13 feet

Rattlesnake

Length: up to 8 feet

RATTLESNAKE

Rattlesnakes inject small animals with **venom** from their fangs, and then swallow them whole!

THE RATTLE!

Like all snakes, rattlesnakes shed their skin from time to time. Each time this happens, a new section is added to their rattle.

The rattlesnake's rattle is made of sections of hard skin at the end of its tail. The rattle warns enemies not to come near.

57

FROGS, TOADS, AND OTHERS

Most amphibians live part of their life in water and part on land. They take in moisture through their skin, so they don't have to drink water.

These are all amphibians.

FROG

Most frogs and toads lay their eggs in water. Toads lay their eggs in long strings, while frogs lay eggs in clusters, called "frog spawn."

The baby frogs, called tadpoles, **hatch** from the frog spawn in a few days.

COMMON FROG

Frog spawn   4 weeks old   12 weeks old   16 weeks old Grown-up!

It can take a few weeks or more than a year for them to turn into frogs.

Some frogs have brightly colored skin to warn **predators** that they are poisonous.

58 The South American poison arrow frog's skin is so deadly that local people use the poison for their arrow tips!

Frogs catch **insects** on their long, sticky tongues. Toads like to eat **insects**, too—and SLUGS!

TOAD

Toads are similar to frogs, but have drier, bumpier skin.

Their hind legs are shorter, too.

HOW BIG ARE THEY?

Frog
Length: ½–15 inches

Toad
Length: 1–10 inches

Newt
Length: 3–10 inches

Salamander
Length: 3–13 inches

SALAMANDER

Salamanders and newts look like lizards, but they don't have scales and they are amphibians.

Most salamanders hide under rocks and leaves during the day and come out at night to feed on **insects**, worms, and snails.

Fire salamander

The giant salamander, which lives in China, is the biggest in the world—it can grow up to 5 feet long.

59

FISH

Fish live in both salt water and **freshwater** all over the world. They can even breathe underwater! They suck in water through their mouths, then push it out through special slits called **gills**. The **gills** help the fish get oxygen out of the water.

GOLDFISH

If goldfish are kept in an indoor aquarium, they stay quite small. But if they live in a pond or stream, where they have lots of room to move about, they can grow to be more than 10 inches long!

Goldfish are not only gold. They can be silvery, white, red, greenish brown, and even black.

Dennis—
Stanley's pet goldfish!

FLYING FISH

To escape from **predators** (like dolphins), the flying fish flaps its tail from side to side to build up speed, whizzes up to the water's surface, launches itself into the air, and then glides on its outstretched fins for more than a quarter mile.

Flying fish don't have wings. They have large, special fins.

60

X-RAY FISH

X-ray fish live in lakes and rivers. They lay hundreds of tiny eggs among the underwater plants.

X-ray fish eat **insects** and **plankton**.

The tiny X-ray fish gets its name from its see-through body!

HOW BIG ARE THEY?

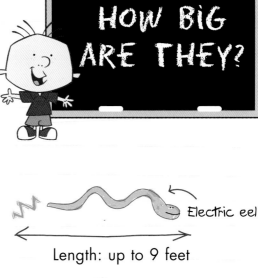

Electric eel

Length: up to 9 feet

Flying fish

Length: up to 9 inches

Goldfish

Length: 3 inches (average)

Clown fish

Length: 3 inches

X-ray fish

Length: 2 inches

CLOWN FISH

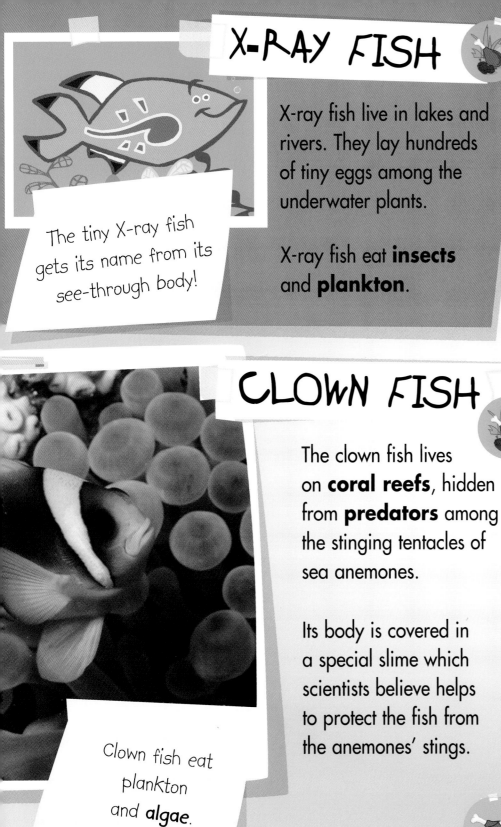

The clown fish lives on **coral reefs**, hidden from **predators** among the stinging tentacles of sea anemones.

Its body is covered in a special slime which scientists believe helps to protect the fish from the anemones' stings.

Clown fish eat plankton and **algae**.

ELECTRIC EEL

Unlike most fish, the electric eel doesn't have scales or **gills**. It comes to the surface to breathe.

Their bodies produce electricity to stun their **prey**. They can even produce a HUGE jolt of electricity that can kill a fish—or even a person!

SHARKS

These fearsome-looking, meat-eating fish live all over the world, mostly in warm seas. People believe that sharks attack humans all the time, but actually there are fewer than 100 shark attacks a year.

GREAT WHITE SHARK

The great white shark has a very good **sense** of smell and is an excellent hunter. It can smell just one drop of blood in 25 gallons of water! Its favorite foods are seals, sea lions, dolphins, and other sharks—but it will eat any creature it can catch!

Some sharks give birth to live babies, called pups. The pups have teeth and start to hunt right away! Great white shark pups are more than 3 feet long when they're born.

Great white sharks have LOTS of teeth. They grow in rows with new ones replacing old ones all the time. A great white shark may grow more than 20,000 new teeth in its lifetime.

A shark's skeleton is made of cartilage, the same bendy stuff that's in your ears and nose!

62

WHALE SHARK

The GIANT whale shark only eats tiny plants and animals called **plankton**.

The whale shark is the biggest fish in the world!

It swims along slowly, filtering the **plankton** from the water through its **gills**.

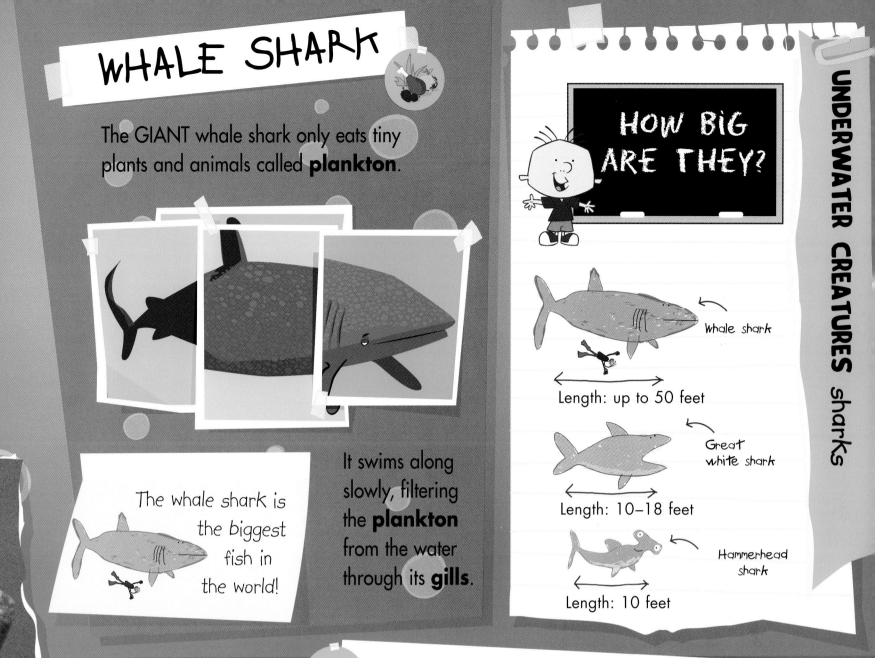

HOW BIG ARE THEY?

Whale shark
Length: up to 50 feet

Great white shark
Length: 10–18 feet

Hammerhead shark
Length: 10 feet

HAMMERHEAD SHARK

The hammerhead's odd head is actually very useful—it helps the shark steer through the water and sense movement around it.

With an eye and a nostril at each end of the "hammer," it can find food over a wider area.

Hammerheads eat fish, squid—and sometimes other sharks!

63

INSIDE-OUT ANIMALS

These amazing creatures are called **crustaceans**, and they all have their skeletons on the outside of their bodies! **Crustaceans** mainly live in the sea, but some live in **freshwater** and even on land.

They have **antennae** and bodies in three sections.

LOBSTER

Lobsters use their tail and five pairs of legs for swimming.

Their huge front legs are snapping claws that they use to defend themselves.

Lobsters crawl along the seabed at night. They eat dead animals and sometimes fish and small sea creatures.

Lobsters can live to be fifty years old.

SHRIMP

Shrimps have five pairs of walking legs and five pairs of swimming legs.

HERMIT CRAB

Unlike other **crustaceans**, hermit crabs don't have their own shells. They use the empty shells of snails or other animals!

Hermit crabs that live near land may even move into coconut shells!

When it gets too big for its home, the hermit crab leaves its shell and moves to a larger one.

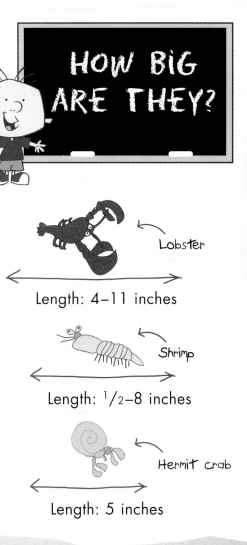

HOW BIG ARE THEY?

Lobster
Length: 4–11 inches

Shrimp
Length: $1/2$–8 inches

Hermit crab
Length: 5 inches

Shrimps live on the floor of oceans and lakes. They eat plants and other small creatures.

Shrimps always swim backward. To swim, they push their abdomen (the middle part of their body) in and out and whip their tail from side to side.

This mantis shrimp has front feeding arms that can move as fast as a bullet! It's much smaller than you, but its arms could smash the bones in your finger!

Shrimps lay as many as 14,000 eggs at a time. The eggs stay attached to the female's legs until they are ready to **hatch**.

65

UNDERWATER ODDITIES

Some of the strangest-looking creatures on Earth live under the sea!

They all do AMAZING stuff!

The giant octopus can grow to 30 feet across.

Octopuses like to eat fish, crabs, lobsters, and other shellfish.

These suckers help it hold on to **prey**.

OCTOPUS

Octopuses have eight armlike tentacles. If they lose a tentacle, they just grow a new one!

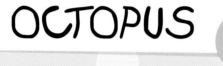

8 1
7   2
6   3
5   4

When a **predator** attacks, the octopus squirts out a black, inky liquid. This makes the water cloudy so the octopus can escape.

JELLYFISH

Its mouth is under here.

SAWFISH

Sawfish use their snouts to dig up their **prey**. Their long, toothy snouts look just like saws.

FLOUNDER

When a flounder is born, it has an eye on each side of its head and looks like a normal fish.

After a few days the fish starts tipping over and swimming on one side. The eye that is underneath moves around to the top side, so both eyes are on the same side!

Baby flounders live near the surface of the sea. When they are grown-up, flounders live on the seabed, searching for small fish to eat.

Jellyfish have no brains, hearts, or bones; they are just made of muscles, nerves, and water!

These tentacles can sting! They help the jellyfish catch its dinner of fish.

Their bodies are see-through, so you can see what they've just had for dinner!

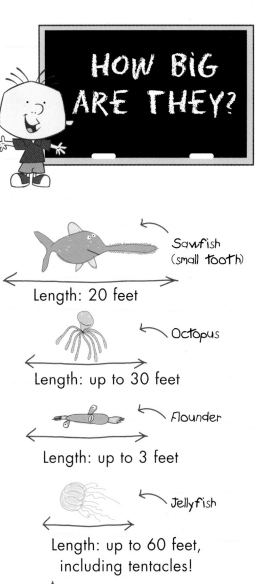

HOW BIG ARE THEY?

Sawfish (small tooth)
Length: 20 feet

Octopus
Length: up to 30 feet

Flounder
Length: up to 3 feet

Jellyfish
Length: up to 60 feet, including tentacles!

Sea horse
Length: up to 8 inches

SEA HORSE

Their bodies are covered in bony armor.

Sea horses are actually fish. They eat **plankton**.

Male sea horses help give birth to their babies! The female lays the eggs in a pouch on the male's front. Dad carries the eggs until they are ready to **hatch**.

67

ANTS

Ants are found all over the world except in Antarctica. Some are meat-eaters, others eat plants, and a few only drink honeydew made by bugs. Most ants cannot see—instead, they release special smells so they can signal to one another! Ants live in big **colonies**, like a huge family.

Looks a bit crowded!

Most of the ants in a colony are "workers." Inside the nest, some workers look after the eggs (which are laid by the queen ant), while others collect food to feed the **larvae**. Some ants are "soldiers"—they defend the nest.

68

Ants can't swallow solid food so they squeeze out the liquid from the food instead.

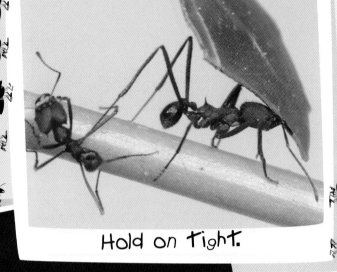

Hold on tight.

HOW BIG ARE THEY?

Army ant
Length: up to 1 inch

Black garden ant
Length: up to 1/10 inch

Ants can lift twenty times their own body weight.

Ants have a stomach (for food for themselves) and a "crop" (a special place inside them) where they can store food to share with the other ants!

Ants are very fast runners. If an ant were the same size as a human, it could run as fast as a racehorse!

Ants can be very clean and tidy. Some ants have a separate chamber in their nest to put waste in. This Keeps it away from the rest of the nest.

I'm glad they're not THIS BIG!

69

HAIRY SPIDERS

You may think spiders are **insects**, but they are actually different creatures, called **arachnids**. There are about 40,000 different types of spider, and they all make silk inside their bodies. Some spiders use the silk to make traps called "webs."

Eight eyes and eight legs!

JUMPING SPIDER

Jumping spiders are very hairy and often brightly colored.

Like all spiders, jumping spiders have eight eyes. Two of them are very big, like car headlights.

Jumping spiders can leap up to 25 times the length of their body—that would be like your jumping the length of five cars!

This is an orb web. You will often see spiders that build orb webs in gardens.

70 Its big eyes help the spider spot the insects it likes to eat from a long way off.

ORB WEB SPIDER

Orb web spiders build circular webs. The spider waits in the center, and when it feels vibrations (little movements) with its feet, it knows that an insect (like a fly) has come into the web.

The spider rushes out and grabs its **prey**. It injects it with **venom**; then it wraps it in silk thread—dinnertime!

FLYING INSECTS

They have wings.

All insects do not live their busy lives on the ground—many also fly.

Butterflies and moths look alike, but butterflies are usually more colorful. Butterflies are active during the day, while most moths are only active at night.

BUTTERFLY

Butterflies and moths both have four life stages:
1: They start off as eggs. 2: Caterpillars hatch out of the eggs. 3: The caterpillars make themselves a cozy shell called a "pupa," and a butterfly or moth grows inside. 4: The butterfly or moth comes out of the pupa and flies away!

Many butterflies can taste with their feet! If a leaf will make tasty food for their babies (the caterpillars), they lay their eggs on it.

FIREFLY

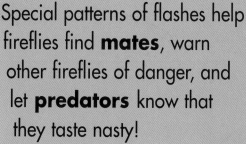

The underside of the firefly's stomach has a special part that lights up.

Special patterns of flashes help fireflies find **mates**, warn other fireflies of danger, and let **predators** know that they taste nasty!

HONEYBEE

Honeybees live in **colonies** in special "bee homes" called hives.

Inside, they build little waxy sections called "cells." The queen bee lays an egg in each cell. The eggs grow into **larvae**, and then the **larvae** become bees.

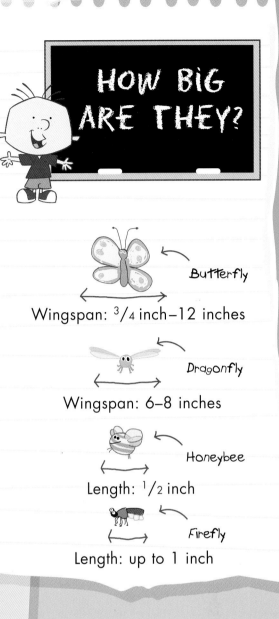

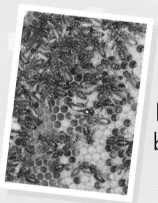

Worker bees collect **nectar** from flowers. They eat the sweet **nectar** and turn it into honey inside their bodies. The bee **larvae** are fed on honey.

HOW BIG ARE THEY?

Butterfly
Wingspan: 3/4 inch–12 inches

Dragonfly
Wingspan: 6–8 inches

Honeybee
Length: 1/2 inch

Firefly
Length: up to 1 inch

DRAGONFLY

Dragonflies live near lakes, ponds, and streams. They can fly faster than 40 mph to catch the small flying insects they eat.

They breathe through holes in their stomachs.

Their huge, bulging eyes can see in all directions.

Young dragonflies are called "nymphs." They live under the water.

73

WORMS AND BEETLES

You've probably seen some of these "creepy crawlies" in a park or in your garden. They work hard, getting rid of pests and garbage and helping things to grow.

STAG BEETLE

Male stag beetles have jaws shaped like a stag's **antlers**. The males use their jaws when they are fighting over females.

Stag beetles are among the biggest beetles in the world. They eat rotting wood and sap (a sticky liquid inside trees).

IMPORTANT NOTE

Stag beetles need rotting wood to eat, but the forests where they live are being cut down. There used to be lots of stag beetles all over the world—now they are endangered.

If a bird comes too close to a ladybug, it will "play dead." Many birds won't eat an insect that isn't moving!

When the weather gets cold, ladybugs keep warm by huddling together in groups of up to 100. In winter they **hibernate**.

LADYBUG

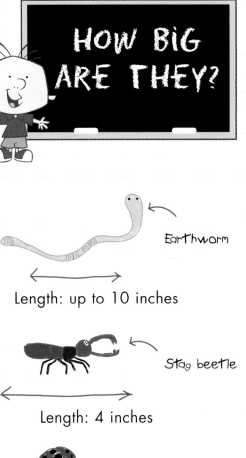

Farmers and gardeners love ladybugs, because they eat aphids, little bugs that damage plants.

The hard shell protects their wings, and the bright red color warns birds that they taste bad!

HOW BIG ARE THEY?

Earthworm
Length: up to 10 inches

Stag beetle
Length: 4 inches

Ladybug
Length: 1/3 inch

EARTHWORM

Earthworms eat rotting leaves and dead parts of plants. They will also eat the rotting remains of animals.

Earthworms cannot see or hear, but they can feel vibrations (small movements).

One type of earthworm in Australia can grow to 10 feet long!

Their waste is called "castings." The castings are filled with **nutrients** which go back into the soil and help to feed plants.

75

SEABIRDS

All these birds are at home on the sea, but they come ashore to build nests and lay their eggs. Penguin moms and dads take turns sitting on the nest or looking for food. Seagulls nest on high, rocky cliffs, or rooftops, and albatrosses set up nesting **colonies** on remote islands where there are no people.

PENGUINS

Penguins eat fish, squid, and **crustaceans**.

Penguins can't fly! They are clumsy on land, but quick and graceful in the water.

Sometimes penguins toboggan across the snow on their bellies—it's easier than walking!

A layer of **blubber** keeps penguins warm.

There may be thousands of baby penguins in a colony, but parents always recognize their own chick by its voice.

These emperor penguins live on the Antarctic ice. The male keeps the egg warm on his feet—under his belly. The egg **hatches** after about two months.

76

ALBATROSS

Sailors used to believe that killing an albatross would bring bad luck.

The wandering albatross has the longest wingspan of any bird—almost 12 feet.

Albatrosses like windy weather. Their long wings make them excellent gliders, and they can float in the air for hours without ever flapping their wings. They only come ashore to breed.

Their favorite foods are fish and squid.

HOW BIG ARE THEY?

Albatross
Wingspan: up to 12 feet

Herring gull
Wingspan: 1–5 feet

Emperor penguins are the tallest!

Penguin
Height: 1–4 feet

SEAGULL

At sea, gulls dive for fish, but closer to the shore they pick up **crustaceans** and **insects** on beaches.

Herring gulls scavenge for food in garbage close to the shore. This can help keep bays and harbors clean, but in some places there are so many gulls that they become a nuisance.

77

HUNTING BIRDS

Small creatures, BEWARE!

Birds that hunt other animals for food are called "birds of **prey**." Owls and eagles both use their strong claws to grab and kill their **prey**.

 ## OWL

With their soft feathers, owls make no noise when they fly.

Most owls are **nocturnal**. They hunt for mice and other small mammals at night.

Owls have better hearing than any other bird. They also have very good eyesight and can turn their heads almost all the way around.

78

The bald eagle is the national bird of the U.S.A.

BALD EAGLE

The big, powerful bald eagle is not really bald—the white feathers on its head make it look bald from far away.

Bald eagles nest in high, hard-to-reach places. They use the same nest over and over, adding more branches and twigs every year. The largest bald eagle nest ever found was 18 feet deep and 9 feet wide!

Bald eagles usually live near water. They grab fish from the surface with their claws. They also eat other birds, small mammals, reptiles and **carrion**.

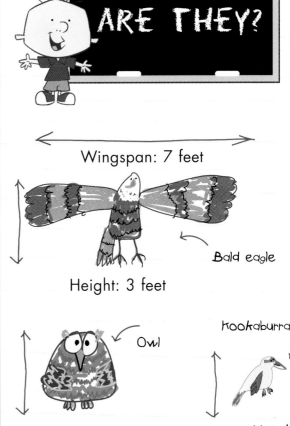

HOW BIG ARE THEY?

Wingspan: 7 feet

Bald eagle

Height: 3 feet

Owl

kookaburra

Height: 6 inches to 2 feet 4 inches

Height: 1 foot 5 inches

KOOKABURRA

Kookaburras use their loud, shrieking call to tell other kookaburras where they are. It sounds like they are laughing!

Ha-ha-ha!

They eat **insects**, worms, and reptiles—even poisonous snakes.

Young kookaburras often help raise their younger brothers and sisters.

79

BIRDS THAT LOVE WATER

Thick, waterproof feathers!

Birds like ducks, swans, and geese are called "waterfowl." They have **webbed** feet for swimming, and their bodies produce special oils that make their feathers water-repellent.

CANADA GOOSE

The female Canada goose builds a nest on the ground, near water. The gander (male) stands guard.

The goslings (babies) grow very quickly.

Canada geese eat grass, seeds, and plants.

In autumn, Canada geese fly south to spend the winter in warmer places. They fly in a V shape, honking as they go!

The lead bird in the V creates a "slipstream"—a stream of air that helps pull all the other birds along. When the lead bird gets tired, one from the back, who has had a rest, takes over.

SWAN

Swans are the fastest swimmers and fastest flyers of all the waterfowl. They eat plants and small underwater creatures.

Cygnets (baby swans) have short necks and fluffy brown or gray feathers.

Biggest waterfowl

Just like in the story *The Ugly Duckling*, it takes a year or two before cygnets turn white.

Cobs (males) and pens (females) pair up and stay together their whole lives.

HOW BIG ARE THEY?

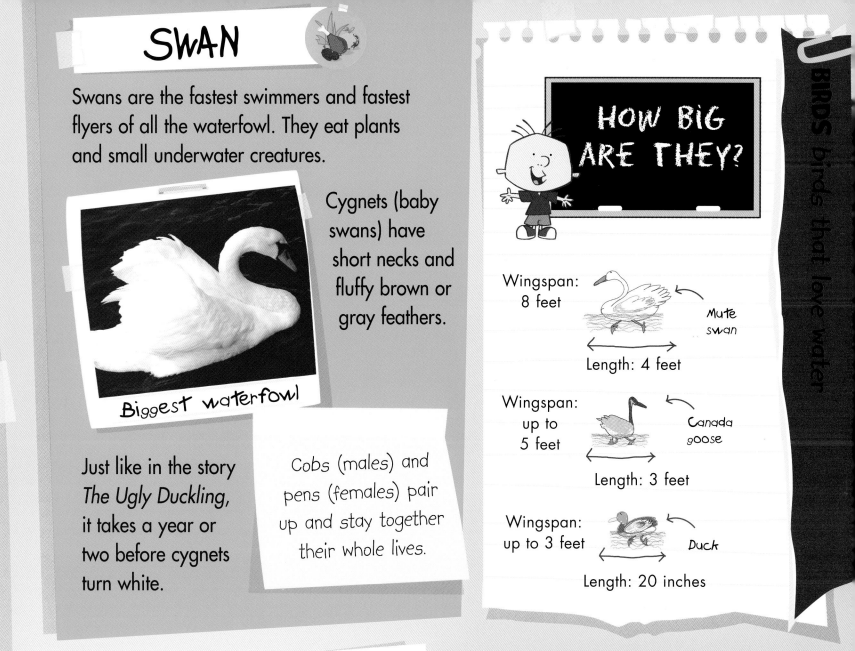

Wingspan: 8 feet
Mute swan
Length: 4 feet

Wingspan: up to 5 feet
Canada goose
Length: 3 feet

Wingspan: up to 3 feet
Duck
Length: 20 inches

DUCKS

The mallard is the wild relative of most **domestic** ducks. The males have colorful feathers, while the females are just brown.

Most **domestic** ducks are white. Males and females look almost the same.

Eiders and scoters are sea ducks. They dive for their food in the sea and eat shellfish and other **crustaceans.**

Mallards eat plants, **insects**, frogs, worms, snails, and slugs!

81

BIRDS WITH SPECIAL TALENTS

All birds can do amazing stuff, but these unusual birds have skills that make them extra special!

Good at pecking and running!

UMBRELLA BIRD

The umbrella bird lives in tall rain-forest trees. It likes to eat fruit.

When a male umbrella bird wants to attract a **mate**, he spreads out the tuft of feathers on his head. It looks just like an umbrella!

Umbrella birds also have "wattles"—folds of skin hanging from their throats, like those of a turkey.

IMPORTANT NOTE

The umbrella bird is under threat because it is losing its habitat. The rain-forest trees that it lives in are being cut down by people who want to sell the wood, or who need to clear the land so that they can grow food.

ROADRUNNER

Roadrunners eat lizards, snakes, birds, and small animals—they spear them with their beaks!

Long legs make roadrunners very speedy. They race along at up to 15 mph.

82

WOODPECKER

Most woodpeckers peck holes in trees to find **insects** to eat.

Their stiff tail feathers and strong feet keep them upright while they peck at tree trunks.

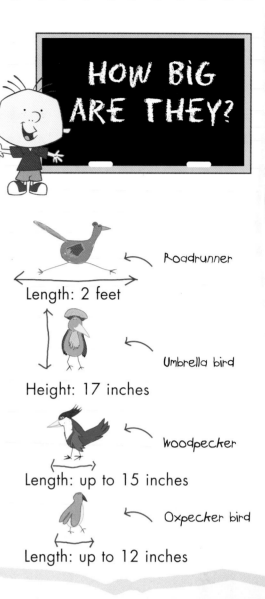

HOW BIG ARE THEY?

Roadrunner
Length: 2 feet

Umbrella bird
Height: 17 inches

Woodpecker
Length: up to 15 inches

Oxpecker bird
Length: up to 12 inches

When they sense danger, roadrunners crouch and try to hide. But if they need to escape from a **predator**, they can make a fast getaway.

Their long, narrow tails help the birds to balance and make speedy turns while they're running.

OXPECKER BIRD

Their sharp nails help them cling to the animals' backs.

Oxpeckers are also called "tickbirds."

They perch on big mammals such as cattle, rhinos, and elephants, and eat the annoying ticks and flies.

When two creatures help each other in this way, they are called **symbionts**.

83

BIRDS THAT SING

Most birds sing to attract a **mate**, or to tell other birds where their **territory** is. The mockingbird copies the songs of other birds and can even make sounds like a dog bark or piano music!

Pop stars of the bird world!

 ## MOCKINGBIRD

Mother mockingbirds are so protective, they will even attack cats or people if they think their eggs or babies are in danger.

They like to eat fruit, grasshoppers, beetles, spiders, lizards, and snakes!

They build bowl-shaped nests made of twigs and grass.

Mockingbirds can sing for hours at a time.

CARDINAL

Male and female cardinals sing to each other all year long. They are especially loud just before nesting time, in the spring.

The male cardinal is easy to spot with his bright red feathers. Females have some red feathers, too, but they are mostly dull brown and gray.

Cardinals like to eat seeds, insects, snails, and the sap (sticky juice) from maple trees.

HOW BIG ARE THEY?

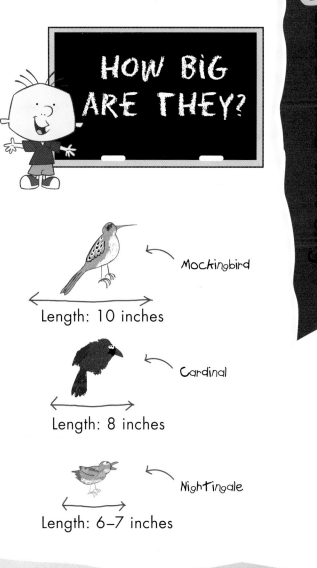

Mockingbird
Length: 10 inches

Cardinal
Length: 8 inches

Nightingale
Length: 6–7 inches

NIGHTINGALE

Nightingales mainly sing at night. Their song is loud with a beautiful tune, but they are quite shy—so it is hard to spot them.

Nightingales eat **insects**, worms, spiders, berries, and fruit.

When males are trying to find a **mate**, they sing all day and all night. They only stop singing when a female joins them.

Nightingales nest near the ground. Their nests are made of twigs and lined with grass.

BIG BIRDS

Some birds are taller than you. Ostriches are even bigger than your mom and dad. They are the world's biggest birds!

OSTRICH

The ostrich's long, thin neck makes up almost half its height.

Ostriches cannot fly, but to escape a **predator**, they can run very fast—up to 45 mph.

Ostriches live in large herds, searching for their favorite foods—plants and grass.

Several females in a herd will share a nest and lay their eggs together.

Ostrich eggs are about the size of a honeydew melon—the biggest egg in the animal kingdom.

86

When the eggs **hatch**, Dad looks after the babies.

FLAMINGO

Flamingos live in huge flocks in "wetlands" (places with lots of shallow water). Sometimes there are as many as a million birds in a flock!

The American flamingos' pink color comes from the shrimp they eat. Without it, their feathers would turn white.

Flamingos can stand on one leg for ages, even when they're asleep! This stops them from losing too much heat from their legs and feet.

HOW BIG ARE THEY?

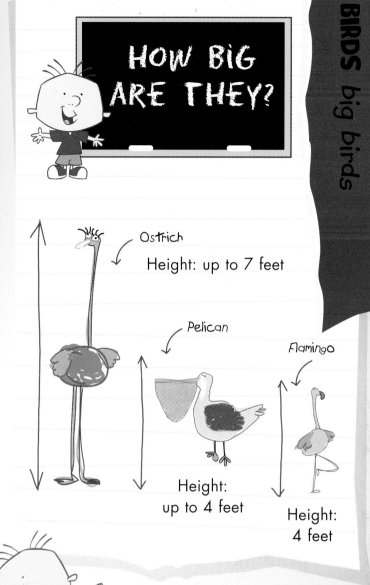

Ostrich
Height: up to 7 feet

Pelican

Flamingo

Height: up to 4 feet

Height: 4 feet

PELICAN

Pelicans have a big, stretchy throat pouch. They scoop up lots of water in the pouch, then strain out the liquid and swallow any fish that are left inside.

Dalmatian pelicans fish in groups. They form a line and chase small fish into shallow water; then they scoop them up and eat them.

The North American brown pelican dives straight down into the sea to catch fish.

87

COLORFUL BIRDS

With their brilliantly colored feathers, these birds stand out from the rest of the flock!

PEAFOWL

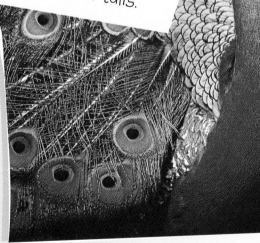

HUMMINGBIRD

Hummingbird wings beat extremely fast. This allows the bird to hover over flowers. The bird positions its long, specially shaped beak in the flower and licks out the **nectar** with its tongue.

They blend in with the flowers, making it hard for **predators** to see them.

Hummingbirds are the smallest birds in the world!

Only the peacocks (male peafowl) have long colorful tails.

PARROT

This colorful scarlet macaw lives high in the rain-forest treetops. It can live to be 80 years old.

IMPORTANT NOTE
*Many parrots are **endangered**. Their forest homes are cut down, and the birds are captured to be sold as pets!*

88

All parrots have strong, hooked beaks and muscular tongues that they use to break into fruits and seeds. They eat **nectar** and insects, too.

Peafowl eat seeds, fruit, plants, and **insects**. They feed on the ground, but sleep in trees.

BLUEBIRD

In some parts of North America, the arrival of the bluebird from its winter home in the South is a sure sign that spring is coming.

Bluebirds build their nests in holes in trees or fences.

They feed on butterflies, beetles, spiders, and small insects.

HOW BIG ARE THEY?

Peacock
Body length: 3 feet 4 inches

Parrot
Length: up to 3 feet

Bluebird
Length: 8 inches

Chicken
Height: 2 feet

Hummingbird
Length: 2 1/2–7 inches

CHICKEN

comb

wattle

Roosters (adult male chickens) and cockerels (young male chickens) are more brightly colored than hens (females).

They have larger combs and **wattles**, and longer tail feathers, too.

"cock-a-doodle-doo"

The peacock displays his tail in a wide fan when he wants to attract a peahen (female).

The rooster's crow attracts females, warns off other males, and awakens humans.

89

SCAVENGER BIRDS

They eat leftovers!

Scavengers are birds (or other animals) that eat whatever they can find!

CITY PIGEON

City pigeons nest on bridges or buildings, and in little holes or on ledges.

Speedy pigeons can fly 60 mph! That's the speed of a car on a highway!

Wild pigeons are not normally scavengers.

But city pigeons eat leftover food they find on pavements and in parks.

City pigeons are descended from rock doves—wild pigeons that nest on cliffs.

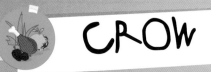

CROW

Crows like to eat **carrion**, as well as fruit, **insects**, corn, and grain.

RAVEN

Ravens are the biggest member of the crow family. With their glossy blue-black feathers, black feet, and large beaks, ravens can look scary.

They eat almost anything, including seeds, berries, and garbage!

Ravens are very clever. Young birds can sometimes be taught to copy human speech.

Some farmers put up scarecrows to "scare crows" away from their crops.

Sometimes crows live in huge flocks. While the rest of the birds eat, one or two look out for danger.

HOW BIG ARE THEY?

Vulture
Length: up to 3 feet

Raven
Length: 2 feet

Crow
Length: 18 inches

Pigeon
Length: 12 inches

VULTURE

Vultures sometimes hunt live **prey**, but mostly they help themselves to other animals' leftovers!

Their strong beaks are good at tearing.

91

GLOSSARY

ALGAE A type of simple plant, such as pond scum, algae has no stems, flowers, or leaves.

ANTENNAE A pair of movable feelers on the head of an insect or crustacean.

ANTLERS A pair of hornlike growths on the head of some deer. Antlers sometimes look like tree branches!

AQUATIC An animal or bird that lives most or all of its life in or on the water.

ARACHNIDS Creatures, including spiders and ticks, with four pairs of legs.

BLOWHOLES Openings at the top of the head that cetaceans (aquatic mammals) use to breathe through when they come to the surface.

BLUBBER A thick layer of fat under the skin that keeps an animal warm.

BURROW A hole or tunnel that an animal digs in the ground to use as its home, or as a shelter.

CAMOUFLAGE Colorings or markings on an animal that help it hide or blend in with its surroundings. Camouflage is a good way to hide from predators, as well as a handy method to stop prey from seeing you coming!

CARNIVORES Animals that only eat meat or fish.

CARRION Dead animals.

CETACEANS Aquatic mammals (like whales and dolphins) that live underwater, but need to come to the surface to breathe.

COLONIES Groups of animals that live together.

CONSERVATION Preserving and protecting the environment and its natural resources.

CORAL REEFS Huge, underwater places that look like they are made from rocks, but are actually made from the bodies of coral animals called "polyps." Polyps have hard outer skeletons that link to the skeleton of other polyps on a coral reef. When a polyp dies, its skeleton stays as part of the reef, so the reefs keep getting bigger.

CRUSTACEANS Aquatic animals, such as lobsters and crabs. They have hard, outer shells instead of a skeleton; bodies in sections; and jointed legs.

DOMESTIC Animals that live with people. Pets and farm animals are domestic animals.

ENDANGERED When the number of a species of animal becomes very low, and the remaining animals are in danger of being eliminated by humans or losing their natural habitat (the place where they live).

FANGS Very sharp teeth used by mammals for grabbing prey and tearing meat. Snakes' fangs are hollow (like little tubes) and are used to inject venom.

FRESHWATER Rainwater and the water in lakes, ponds, rivers, and streams. It is not salty.

GILLS Special organs in the bodies of fish and some amphibians. The gills take oxygen out of the water and send it into the animal's body so that it can breathe.

HATCH To be born by breaking out of an egg.

HERBIVORES Animals that only eat plants.

HIBERNATION Spending most or all of the winter sleeping, while food is scarce. Some hibernating animals, such as the grizzly bear and the groundhog, live off their body fat.

INSECTS Tiny creatures with bodies in three sections and three pairs of legs. Many insects have wings, too.

LARVAE The young of many kinds of insects.

MARINE Having to do with the sea; marine mammals are mammals that live in the sea.

MARSUPIALS Animals best known for carrying their newborn babies in a pouch (pocket) outside their body until the babies are big enough to look after themselves.

MATE When a male and female animal come together to produce babies. It is also the word used for an animal's partner.

NECTAR A sweet liquid made by plants. Bees use it to make honey, and many other insects and birds eat it.

NOCTURNAL When an animal is active only at night.

NUTRIENTS A substance or ingredient found in food that nourishes animals and plants.

OMNIVORES Animals that eat both meat (or fish) and plants.

PLANKTON Microscopic (very, very tiny) plants and animals that live in the sea and in lakes.

PREDATORS Animals that hunt and kill other animals for food.

PREY An animal that is hunted by another animal for food.

PRIMATES An animal group that includes monkeys and apes. Humans are primates, too.

SCENT GLANDS Organs (parts) of an animal's body that secrete a smelly scent.

SENSES Hearing, seeing, smelling, tasting, and touching—the way animals get information from the world around them.

SWAMP Very wet areas with lots of water plants.

SYMBIONTS Animals from different species that live together closely and cooperate with one another.

TERRITORY The area that one animal defends against other animals to keep its food supply and family safe.

TUSKS Very long, pointed teeth that grow out of an animal's face or mouth.

VENOM A poison produced in the bodies of some animals, such as snakes and spiders.

WATTLE A fleshy piece found around the head or neck of a bird or animal.

WEBBED Feet of various birds and animals where the toes are joined together by a flap of skin.

93

BABY ANIMAL NAMES

Alligator: hatchling

Anteater: young/baby

Antelope: calf

Ape: infant/young

Armadillo: young/baby

Bald eagle: eaglet

Bat: pup

Bear: cub

Beaver: kitten/pup

Bird (*Albatross; bluebird; cardinal; chicken; crow; flamingo; kookaburra; hummingbird; mockingbird; nightingale; ostrich; oxpecker; parrot; pelican; penguin; raven; seagull; umbrella bird; vulture; woodpecker*): chick

Butterfly: caterpillar

Camel: calf

Cheetah: cub

Cow: calf

Crab: larva

Crocodile: hatchling

Dolphin: calf

Domestic dog: puppy

Dragonfly: nymph

Duck: duckling

Earthworm: baby earthworm

Electric eel: elver

Elephant: calf

Firefly: larva

Fish: fry/minnow

Flying squirrel: baby flying squirrel

Fox: kit/cub/pup

Frog: tadpole

Giraffe: calf

Goat: kid

Goose: gosling

Groundhog: kit/cub

Hedgehog: piglet

Hippopotamus: calf

Honeybee: larva

Horse: foal

Ibex: kid

Jackrabbit (*hare*): leveret

Jellyfish: ephyna

Kangaroo: joey

Koala: joey

Ladybug: larva

Leopard: cub

Lion: cub

Lizard: baby lizard

Lobster: larva

Manatee: calf

Monkey: infant

Moose: calf

Mouse: kitten

Octopus: baby octopus

Owl: owlet/howlet

Peafowl: peachick

Pig: piglet

Pigeon: squab

Platypus: puggle

Porcupine: baby porcupine/porcupette

Prairie dog: young

Rabbit: kitten/bunny

Raccoon: cub

Reindeer: fawn

Rhinoceros: calf

Ring-tailed lemur: infant

Salamander: larva

Sea lion: pup

Sea otter: pup/ kitten/cub

Sea horse: sea pony

Seal: pup

Shark: pup

Shrimp: larva

Skunk: kitten

Sloth: young/baby

Snake: baby snake

Spider: spiderling

Squirrel: kitten/pup

Stag beetle: grub

Swan: cygnet

Tasmanian devil: cub

Tiger: cub

Toad: tadpole

Tortoise: hatchling

Turtle: hatchling

Vole: baby vole

Walrus: cub

Whale: calf

Wild boar: boarlet/piglet

Wolf: cub

Yak: calf

Zebra: foal

INDEX

INDEX